Dear Parents and Educators,

Welcome to Penguin Young Readers! As parents and educators, you know that each child develops at his or her own pace—in terms of speech, critical thinking, and, of course, reading. Penguin Young Readers recognizes this fact. As a result, each Penguin Young Readers book is assigned a traditional easy-to-read level (1–4) as well as a Guided Reading Level (A–P). Both of these systems will help you choose the right book for your child. Please refer to the back of each book for specific leveling information. Penguin Young Readers features esteemed authors and illustrators, stories about favorite characters, fascinating nonfiction, and more!

Llama Llama™: Llama Llama, Be My Valentine!

LEVEL **2**

GUIDED READING LEVEL **I**

This book is perfect for a **Progressing Reader** who:
- can figure out unknown words by using picture and context clues;
- can recognize beginning, middle, and ending sounds;
- can make and confirm predictions about what will happen in the text; and
- can distinguish between fiction and nonfiction.

Here are some **activities** you can do during and after reading this book:
- Problem/Solution: In this story, Gilroy Goat is worried because he does not know what to make as a Valentine's gift for his friends. This is the problem. Discuss the solution to Gilroy's problem and how Llama Llama is able to help his friend.
- Make Connections: Gilroy tries many different creative projects to figure out what he is best at. Discuss your favorite creative projects. What are you best at?

Remember, sharing the love of reading with a child is the best gift you can give!

—Sarah Fabiny, Editorial Director
   Penguin Young Readers program

*Penguin Young Readers are leveled by independent reviewers applying the standards developed by Irene Fountas and Gay Su Pinnell in *Matching Books to Readers: Using Leveled Books in Guided Reading*, Heinemann, 1999.

PENGUIN YOUNG READERS
An Imprint of Penguin Random House LLC

Penguin supports copyright. Copyright fuels creativity, encourages diverse voices,
promotes free speech, and creates a vibrant culture. Thank you for buying an authorized edition
of this book and for complying with copyright laws by not reproducing, scanning, or distributing
any part of it in any form without permission. You are supporting writers and allowing Penguin
to continue to publish books for every reader.

Copyright © Anna E. Dewdney Literary Trust. Copyright © 2018 Genius Brands International, Inc.
Published by Penguin Young Readers, an imprint of Penguin Random House LLC,
345 Hudson Street, New York, New York 10014. Manufactured in China.

ISBN 9781524789190 (pbk)   10 9 8 7 6 5 4 3 2 1
ISBN 9781524788957 (hc)   10 9 8 7 6 5 4 3 2 1

llama llama™
Anna Dewdney
be my valentine!

based on the bestselling children's book series
by Anna Dewdney

Penguin Young Readers
An Imprint of Penguin Random House

Llama Llama
is at school.
He is happy.
Tomorrow is
Valentine's Day!
He jumps for joy.

4

Zelda Zebra

is Llama Llama's teacher.

"Valentine's Day is a day to share

how much you care,"

says Zelda Zebra.

"To celebrate, we are going to have a party!"

says Zelda Zebra.

Each person in Llama's class

will make a special gift

to bring to the party.

It is time to have fun and

be creative!

Zelda Zebra tells everyone

to make something that

only *they* can make.

Luna Giraffe is busy

with her crafts.

She uses glitter,

ribbon, and colored

paper.

Gilroy Goat looks sadly at
his friend Luna.

"I have no idea what gift
to make," he says.

"I'm not very good with glitter."

Gilroy is worried.

What will he make for
his friends?

Llama Llama can help.
"There are so many
other things to make,"
says Llama.

How about a
sculpture from clay?

Oh no!

"I made a blob," says Gilroy.

"Maybe I should try something

besides art," he says.

Llama Llama goes home
after school.
He wants to make his Valentine's
gifts with Mama Llama.

Llama Llama invites Gilroy

to his house to help.

Maybe that will give Gilroy a new

idea of something he can make.

Llama says that he has an idea.

Llama wants to make yummy

cookies for his friends.

"I can make them

heart-shaped!"

he says.

"I'm ready to help,"

says Mama Llama.

"Me too!" shouts Gilroy.

Uh-oh!

Making cookies isn't so easy.

"Our cookies look like blobs!"

says Llama Llama.

Mama Llama has an idea.

"I say we make another batch,"

she says.

Next time they

will look like

hearts.

Llama Llama and Gilroy take a
break from baking to visit Luna.
She is making animals out of
paper for her gifts.
"I knew you would make
something fantastic!"
says Llama Llama.
"You are always so creative!"

The boys try to make

a paper bird.

Oh no!

Gilroy's bird doesn't look like

a bird at all!

"I better keep trying to find

something else I'm good at,"

says Gilroy.

At home, Llama Llama and

Gilroy make another batch

of cookies.

Oh no!

These cookies do not look like

hearts, either!

"This cookie looks like an octopus!" Llama says as he looks at his cookies.

"Don't worry.

We will try again," says Mama.

"While these cookies are baking, let's go visit Nelly to see what she is making,"

says Llama.

Llama and Gilroy go to

Nelly's house.

"It smells so good in here!"

says Gilroy.

"We're using cookie cutters to

make chocolate shapes,"

says Nelly.

Nelly came up

with a great gift!

Gilroy tries to make
a chocolate shape.

Gilroy makes a mess instead.

"Don't worry, Gilroy.

I know you'll find the right thing

to make," says Nelly.

On the way home, Llama Llama
and Gilroy visit Euclid.
Euclid is making little buildings
out of wooden sticks.
Wow!

"These buildings
are so amazing!"
says Llama Llama.

But Gilroy can't build anything

like that for his friends.

He is not great at math

like Euclid is.

"You have to figure out your *own*

thing," says Llama Llama.

"I know that you will come up

with something great!"

says Euclid.

The Valentine's Day party is finally here!

"What amazing and original valentines!" says Zelda Zebra.

"I made heart-shaped cookies for everyone," says Llama Llama.

"You just have to use your imagination on the heart part!" he says.

Everyone laughs and eats a cookie.

There is one more gift to give out.

It is a Valentine's Day card.

But these aren't just *any*

Valentine's Day cards.

There are

poems inside!

Llama Llama reads his card
out loud.

It says he is a great friend.

"I love my poem!" he says.

"Did you get a poem, Gilroy?"

asks Luna.

Gilroy shrugs.

Wait!

Llama Llama understands.

"It was *you*!

You wrote the poems!"

Llama Llama shouts.

"This is what you made for

Valentine's Day," he says.

Gilroy smiles proudly.

"You told me to do something

that was creative and *me*!

And I love writing!" he says

to Zelda Zebra.

"And you are so good at it!

I hope you do a lot more

of it," says Zelda Zebra.

What a special Valentine's Day.

Llama Llama and his classmates

show one another

how much they care—

and they discover their own

special talents!